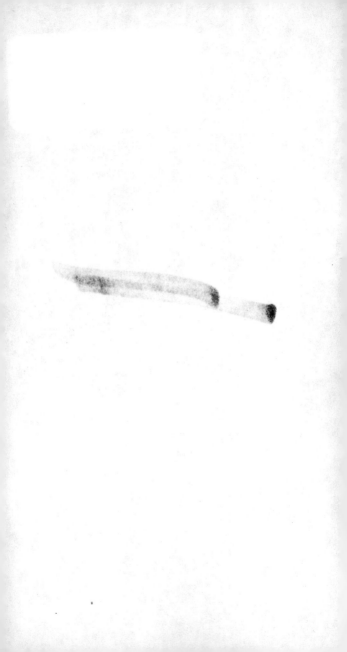

NOBODY KNOWS

Tana Reiff

A Pacemaker® **HOPES** *And* **DREAMS** Book

FEARON/JANUS/QUERCUS
Belmont, California

Simon & Schuster Supplementary Education Group

HOPES *And* DREAMS

Hungry No More
For Gold and Blood
O Little Town
Push to the West
Nobody Knows
Old Ways, New Ways
Little Italy
A Different Home
Boat People
The Magic Paper

Cover photo: Library of Congress
Illustration: Tennessee Dixon

Copyright © 1989 by FEARON/JANUS/QUERCUS,
a division of Simon & Schuster Supplementary Education
Group, 500 Harbor Boulevard, Belmont, California 94002
All rights reserved. No part of this book may be reproduced
by any means, transmitted, or translated into a machine
language without written permission from the publisher.

ISBN 0-8224-3683-3
Library of Congress
Catalog Card Number: 87-83216
Printed in the United States of America
10 9 8 7

CONTENTS

CHAPTER 1
The American South, 1902

Mama came in
from the fields.
The day was hot.
Six-year-old Mattie
was shelling peas.
She looked up
at her mother.
Mama looked tired.

"Finish up, child!"
said Mama.
"We are going
into town.
I'll get
the horse and wagon ready.
Hurry up!"

Mattie finished
the basket of peas

as fast as she could.
She loved
going into town
with Mama.
It was fun
to get off the farm
now and then.

Mama lifted Mattie
onto the wagon.
She talked
the whole way to town.
"If you're a good girl,
I'll buy you
a sweet,"
she told Mattie.

Of course,
Mattie was good.
After shopping,
Mama took her
to the sweet shop.

The shop
had two doors.
The first door

had fresh paint.
The second door
was old and worn.
"White Only,"
said the sign
on the first door.
"Colored Only,"
said the sign
on the second door.
Mattie and Mama
went in
the second door.

Inside, Mr. Prinn
was serving
some white people.
Mattie and Mama waited
on the other side
of the sweet shop.

Another white woman
came in after them.
Mr. Prinn
served her.
Mattie and Mama
still waited.

At last,
Mr. Prinn
came over
to Mattie and Mama.

"We'll each have
a soft drink,"
said Mama.
"And a sweet roll
for the little one."

Mr. Prinn
brought them
their order.
He never cracked a smile
or said a word.

"I don't think
that man likes us,"
said Mattie.

"Don't mind him,"
said Mama.
"Our money
is as good
as any white people's.

Be glad
you're here, child.
I remember
when I was your age.
I was a slave.
My family
was owned
by white people.
They forced us
to stay on their land.
My parents worked
almost all the time.
We couldn't
just take off
for town.
You're lucky, child.
You're free
to come and go."

    "Yes, Mama,"
said Mattie.

Thinking It Over

1. Do you think
   Mama and Mattie
   are lucky?

2. Why do you think
   the shop
   has one part for whites
   and one for blacks?

3. How important is it
   to be able to come and go
   as you please?

CHAPTER 2

Over the years
Mattie grew
tall and strong.
But the farm
earned less money every year.
Mama and Daddy
could never get ahead.
They were supposed
to pay their rent
in cotton.
But some years
they didn't grow enough
to cover the rent.

Mattie and the other children
all worked
on the farm.
The land
was not their own.
It never would be.

But the whole family
put their hearts
into every inch of ground.

When Mattie was 18
she met Nate Charles.
He was a big man
and a good farmer.
He worked hard,
just like Mama and Daddy.
He rented a farm
about ten miles south.

"Marry me,"
he begged Mattie.
"I'll give you
the best life
I can.
I can't give you
a gold ring.
But we can have
a fine little wedding.
Be my wife, Mattie."

Mattie said yes.
They held

a nice wedding
in the country church.

"Not like your grandmother,"
said Mama.
"She and your grandfather
were married,
all right.
But they never had
any real papers.
Slaves couldn't have
real papers.
You're lucky, child.
You and Nate
are man and wife,
right by law."

Mattie and Nate
began their life
on the farm.
They paid their rent
with a share of the crops.
But they had
a hard time, too.
The cotton crop
was in big trouble.

Every year,
tiny black bugs
called weevils
ate most of it.

One day
Nate was in town.
As he walked
down the street,
a man stopped him.

"I'm from up north,"
said the man.
"I'm looking
for strong men.
Do you want
to make a lot of money?
Then come with me.
I'll even give you
a train ticket.
You can work
in the meat house.
You can live
real well in Chicago.
You'll never live
that well here!"

Thinking It Over

1. What is your idea
   of a "fine wedding"?

2. Is it a good idea
   to move
   to where the jobs are?

CHAPTER 3

Nate told Mattie
about the man
from up north.

"I don't know
about the big city,"
said Mattie.
"I've lived
in the South
all my life.
I'm a farm girl."

"There's work
in Chicago,"
said Nate.
"And there's no cotton
down here.
That's how
I see it."

Mattie wasn't so sure
about the man
from Chicago.
How could they
trust him?
He sounded to her
like the sea captains
Mama had told her about.

A hundred years ago
the captains sailed
to Africa.
They took
strong young Africans
from their homes.
They took them
to America
to become slaves.
They tied their hands
with chains.
They packed them
onto the ships.
Twice a day
they let the Africans
come up on deck
for air.

Other than that,
the Africans
had to sit or lie down.
There was no room
to stand up.

Many of the Africans
got sick.
Some died.
Some went mad.

Months later,
the ships
landed in America.
The Africans were sold
on the block
like animals.

"This young man
is strong as an ox.
How much do I hear
for him?"
a man would call.
White people
might pay $1,800
for a fit slave.

Mattie pictured herself
up on the block.
What would that feel like?
Her grandmother's mother
must have known.
Did she feel
like a piece of meat?

"What are you thinking, girl?"
asked Nate.
"The man from Chicago
is not a slave captain.
This is 1917.
There are
no slaves now
in America."

He talked Mattie
into moving north.
He told her
they would never
be slaves.

Thinking It Over

1. Are you ever afraid
   that a very bad thing
   will happen again?

2. How would you feel
   if you were sold
   like an animal?

CHAPTER 4

Back home,
Mattie saw green fields
out her window.
Here in Chicago,
she saw gray walls.
Back home,
the air was fresh.
Here in the big city,
the air was dirty
and it often
had a bad smell.
Cars raced by
all night long.
The noise
kept Mattie awake.

Nate went to work
in the meat house.
Animals were
brought in there
and hung on big hooks.

Nate cut them up
into pieces of meat.
He had to be careful
not to cut himself.
He worked long hours.
He worked
even if he was very tired.

"Now I know
how the slaves felt,"
said Mattie.

"What do you mean?"
wondered Nate.

"Oh, you know,"
said Mattie.
"I feel like
we were brought
to a strange land.
This place
is nothing like home.
And the work you do—
it's no better
than slave work.
You work

more than any person
should have to.
It's very hard on you.
And your hard work
only helps white people
make money."

   "Oh, no,"
said Nate.
"You must
remember two things.
We get paid.
The slaves did not.
We are free.
The slaves were not.
As a matter of fact,
a lot of the men
I work with
happen to be white.
They do the same job
as I do.
The other day
two of them
were working
next to me.
I heard them

talking about themselves.
They came here
from Poland.
From across the ocean.
They are looking
for a better life,
just like we are."

"I guess you're right,"
said Mattie.
"We did the same thing
when we came to Chicago
from way down South.
We want a better life, too."

In the next two years,
Mattie and Nate
had two children.
They found
a bigger place
to live.
It was clean and nice.
But it was
in a white part of town.
There were
only a few blacks

living there.
The white people
gave Mattie and Nate
mean looks.
The white neighbors
did not want
to live near blacks.

Then one day
there was trouble.
A little black boy
was swimming
in the lake.
Some white people
felt the lake
was theirs.
Some of them
began to throw stones
at the little boy.
He tried to swim away.
But he couldn't.
The stones
kept on hitting him.
His head
went under water.
He never came up.

A big fight
broke out.
Word got around
that there was trouble
at the lake.

"We can't
put up with this!"
said Nate.
"White people
don't have to like us.
But I get angry
when they hurt a child."

Nate headed
for the door.

"Don't go
to the lake!"
Mattie begged.
"You could get hurt!"

"I have to stand up
to this!"
said Nate.
And he was gone.

Thinking It Over

1. Would you be willing
   to move very far away
   from your home
   to get a better life?

2. Should people live
   where they want to?

3. Is there anything
   you are willing
   to stand up for?

CHAPTER 5

Nate ran
toward the lake.
He was big,
and he ran fast.

Mattie took a child
by each hand.
The three of them
ran after Nate.
Mattie spotted Nate
way ahead of her.
But she couldn't
catch up.
The children
couldn't run
fast enough.

A big crowd
was gathering
by the lake.

"Nate! Nate!"
called Mattie.

She saw
her husband's head
above the crowd.
The crowd
got very loud.
A fight
broke out.
Blacks and whites
hit each other.
Mattie lost sight
of Nate's head.

"Nate!"
Mattie cried.
"Where are you?"

Nate couldn't hear her
above the crowd.
The noise
was much too loud.

The fighting
made Mattie think.

She remembered
another of Mama's stories.
One time
some slaves
tried to escape.
They killed
slave owners.
Then they took off
into the night.
But they got caught.
The white men
hung the slaves
from trees.

"The whites
found every way
to keep us down,"
Mama had told her.
"They made
the slaves afraid.
Not many slaves
tried to escape
after that."

Mattie was afraid.
Was Nate all right?

All she could do
was look for him.

At last
the fight
died down.
Most of the people
left the beach.
A few people
lay on the beach.
They were hurt.

Mattie and the children
walked closer
to the water.
Mattie looked
at every hurt black man.
Then she saw him.
Nate was face down
in the sand.

Thinking It Over

1. Why does Mattie
   always remember
   Mama's stories
   about the slaves?

2. Would you be willing
   to get hurt
   for something
   you believed in?

CHAPTER 6

Mattie felt
Nate's chest.
His heart
was beating.
But there was blood
all over him.
Someone had hit him
with a bottle.
Mattie was glad
she had not seen him
go down.
She tore off
a piece of her dress.
She wet it
with water
from the lake.
She wiped the blood
off her husband.

The water
woke Nate up.

"Oh, my mouth!"
he cried.

Mattie wiped off
his mouth.
Then she saw
that two teeth
were gone.
"Dear heart,"
cried Mattie.
"What have they done
to you?"

Nate stood up.
He felt dizzy.
Mattie and the children
helped him walk home.

There, at the front door,
stood five white men
blocking their way.

"Let us pass!"
called Mattie.
"We have
a hurt man here."

One of the men
put his arm
on the door handle.
"You're not
coming in here!"
he said.

"This is our home!"
said Mattie.

"You don't belong here,"
said another white man.
"You people
should stick
to your own part of town."

Just then,
a white neighbor
came out of the building.
"Let them pass!"
she told the men.
"Can't you see
the man is hurt?"

Mattie and Nate
and the children

walked inside.
The white men
stayed outside.

Nate fell down
on the bed.
"Let's leave
this place!"
he cried.
"We can't live
like this!"

The streets
of Chicago
were full of angry people.
There were fights
all over town
between blacks and whites.
There were fires
and flying rocks
everywhere.
The fighting went on
for 13 days.

"I don't understand
white people,"

said Mattie.
"White people
brought us up here
to work.
Now it's white people
who don't want us here."

It made her think
of the slaves.
White people
brought them
to America
to work.
The Africans came
against their will.
Then white people
treated the slaves
like animals.

When Nate felt better,
the Charles family
left the apartment.
They moved back
to the black part
of town.

Thinking It Over

1. If you were Mattie and Nate, would you move out?

2. What do you think the white people wanted from the black people?

3. Do all white people feel the same way about black people?

CHAPTER 7

Nate missed
a week of work.
He lost
a week's pay.
Mattie wanted him
to see a doctor.
But they didn't have
money for a doctor.

Back at the meat house
the white workers
were talking.
They wanted
a better place
to work.
They wanted
sick pay.
They wanted
overtime pay.
They wanted

to move up
to higher jobs.

The white workers
held a meeting.
They called their group
a union.
Together,
they worked hard
to get the things
they wanted.

"How can I join
the union?"
Nate asked Walt Penny.

"You?"
laughed Walt.
"I don't think
you can join.
I mean,
if it were up to me,
I'd let you in."

"You mean
the union

is only for whites?"
asked Nate.

"It looks that way,"
said Walt.

Nate felt
left out.
He worked
as hard as anyone.
If he was not
in the union,
he could never move up.
He would be
cutting meat
until he died.

He watched
as the white workers
got better jobs
at the meat house.
He watched them
get overtime pay.
He knew
it wasn't fair.
But what could he do?

He talked it over
with the other black workers.

"There is only
one thing to do,"
said Bo Green.
"We'll have to start
our own union!"

And so they did.
The white workers
had their union.
The black workers
had theirs.

"Why must there be
two unions?"
Mattie asked Nate.
"It's like
the two doors
at the sweet shop.
Everyone wants
the sweets.
Why have two doors
that lead
to the same place?"

Thinking It Over

1. Why do you think
   there are "two doors
   that lead
   to the same place"?

2. Do you believe
   in unions?
   Why or why not?

CHAPTER 8

Mattie and Nate
had three more children.
Taking care of
the family
kept Mattie busy.
Nate worked
a lot of overtime.
He made
a better living
than most black men.

The apartment
was small.
It was hot
in the summer.
It was cold
in the winter.

However, Mattie
enjoyed the neighbors.
They were all black.

Almost everyone
was from the South.

As time went on,
restaurants opened.
They served
the kind of food
Mattie had loved
back home.
Much of this food
was even better.
New shops
began to spring up, too.
They sold
the kinds of things
that Mattie needed.
There were
many more shops here
than back home.

And some night spots
opened on the block.
Mattie and Nate
could hear
the best music
in the world.

The city
was beginning to feel
like home
to Mattie.
She was not rich.
But life wasn't bad.

One night
Mattie sat alone.
Nate was at work.
The kids were in bed.
Mattie could hear
the street noise.
She began a letter
to Mama.
She knew
Mama couldn't read it.
Mama had never
gone to school.
But Mattie wrote anyway.
Mama always found someone
to read to her.
And every now and then,
someone wrote a letter
from Mama
to Mattie.

Thinking It Over

1. How do you know
   when life is going well
   for you?

2. What do you like to do
   in your free time?

3. How would you
   keep in touch
   with someone
   who can't read?

CHAPTER 9

Mattie looked
at the clock.
It was almost 12:00.
Where was Nate?
He should have been
home by now.

A few minutes later
Mattie heard footsteps.
It sounded
like one man
helping another man
get up the stairs.
Mattie didn't move.
The steps
came closer and closer.
They stopped
at Mattie's door.
There was a knock.
Mattie was afraid.
She opened the door

only an inch.
She saw Bo Green
from the meat house.
Behind him was Nate.

"He's hurt bad!"
said Bo.

There was a white rag
around Nate's hand.
Mattie screamed.
Nate's blood
was turning the rag red.

"He lost two fingers,"
explained Bo.
"The meat
was coming to Nate
too fast.
He cut
his own hand
instead of the meat."

"The union
got you a company doctor,"
said Mattie.

"Why didn't you
take Nate to him?"

"The doctor
goes home at 5:00,"
said Bo.

"Well, let's get him
to a doctor ourselves!"
Mattie cried.

"The company
won't pay
for an outside doctor,"
Bo told her.

"I don't care!
He has lost
a lot of blood!
Let's go right away!
The children
will be all right.
We must go now!"

Mattie and Bo
each took an arm.

They carried Nate
five blocks.
Nate's head
hung down.
He passed out.

At last
they reached
the doctor's house.
All the lights
were out.
Mattie banged
on the door.
No answer.
She banged again.

Dr. Flowers
came to the door.
He let them in.
He took a look
at Nate's hand.
He said nothing.

"Will he be
all right?"
Mattie asked.

"He has lost
a lot of blood,"
said Dr. Flowers.
"He should be
in the hospital.
But there's no time.
I'll do all I can
right here."

But it was too late.
Cutting off two fingers
should not kill anyone.
Not if he gets
the care he needs.
But it killed
Nate Charles.

Mattie was only 32
when her husband died.
She had five children
to feed.
She had no idea
how she would do it.

Thinking It Over

1. Do all companies
   take care of their workers
   as they should?

2. Do people still die
   because they don't get help
   in time?

3. How can Mattie
   take care of her family
   without a husband?

CHAPTER **10**

For one whole week
Mattie did not leave
the house.
She was so sad
she didn't know
what to do.
Her dear Nate
was gone.
How would she feed
the family?

For the first week,
some neighbors
brought in food.
They helped
to care for the children.
Then the help stopped.
Her neighbors had done
all they could.
Most of them didn't have
enough for themselves.

Mattie Charles
was on her own.

"There is only one thing
to do,"
said Mattie.
"I'll have to find
a job."

She knew
she could get a job
cleaning a white family's house.
But how could six people
live on such low pay?

So Mattie rode a bus
to the big steel mill.
She asked the manager
to give her a job.

"Why should we
give you a job?"
said the manager.
"There are men
who need jobs.

Why should we
take a woman?"

   "Because I will work
as hard as any man,"
said Mattie.
"And because I have
a family to feed,
just like any man."

   Mattie wouldn't give up
until he said yes.
Finally he agreed
to hire her.
Her job
was to clean up
the mill.
She would work
all night.
Her children
could sleep
while she worked.
Then she could be home
during the day.
It didn't leave much time
for Mattie to sleep.

"I'm not
much more than
a cleaning woman!"
Mattie said to herself.
"I'm not much different from
my grandmother
and her mother.
This family
hasn't come very far
in a hundred years,
has it?"

She still heard
Nate's voice
in her head.
"Remember two things,"
he had said.
"We get paid.
The slaves did not.
We are free.
The slaves were not."

But those words
didn't sound
good enough anymore.

Thinking It Over

1. Is getting paid
   and being free
   enough for a person?

2. Do you think
   Mattie has a right
   to be angry?

3. What kind of job
   would you try to get
   if you had a big family
   to feed?

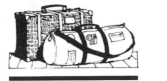

CHAPTER 11

Not long
after Mattie started
at the steel mill,
more trouble began.
It was 1929.
The whole country
began to fall
into the Great Depression.
Some people lost
all their money.
Many people
lost their jobs.
Mattie was afraid
the mill would let her go.

"Last in,
first out!"
was the word.
Those who started last
at the mill
would be the first out.

And Mattie had been
one of the last to start.

"I'm sorry, Mrs. Charles,"
said the manager.
"Our company
can't sell enough steel.
So we don't have work
for everyone.
We must lay you off."

"But I don't make steel,"
said Mattie.
"I'm only
a cleaning woman.
Don't you see?
I have to work
for my children."

"We must put
a steel worker
in your job,"
said the manager.

"You can pay me
ten cents an hour!"

begged Mattie.
"That would be better
than nothing at all!"

She talked the company
into her idea.
But the plan
didn't work for long.
After just three weeks,
she was laid off.

Now there was
only one thing to do.
She took a job
as a maid
for a rich white family.
Every night
she ironed
her black dress
and white blouse.
Every morning
she dressed herself
and the children.

The three older children
were in school.

But each day
one of them
had to stay home.
They took turns
watching the two little ones.

Most nights
Mattie brought home food.
The rich people
didn't know she did it.
Maybe it was wrong,
Mattie sometimes felt.
But five children
needed food.
The rich people
would never miss it.

Then a man
from the school
came to call.
"Your children
are missing
one out of three days,"
he said.
"It is your job

to send them
to school."

"Dear Mama,"
Mattie wrote that night.
"I know
you have lived
all your life
in the South.
But Daddy is gone.
And I need you here.
Please come.
Maybe someday
we can all go home again."

This was not
an easy thing
to ask of Mama.
She was not
young anymore.
But two weeks later
Mama got off the train
in Chicago.

Thinking It Over

1. Would you be willing
   to work for less money
   instead of being laid off?

2. Was Mattie wrong
   to bring the food home?

3. Was Mattie wrong
   to keep her children
   home from school?

4. If you were Mattie,
   would you ask for help?

CHAPTER **12**

For the next 12 years
Mattie worked
as a maid.
Mama helped
to care for the children.
The children grew up.
Mama grew older.
Soon Mattie and her children
had to care for Mama.

The United States
joined the Second World War
in 1941.
Mattie's oldest boy
went off to fight.
He fought
with other black men.
The white men
and black men
did not fight together.
"Why have two doors

that lead
to the same place?"
Mattie wondered again.

When men
went to war,
women went to work.
That was why
Mattie went back
to the steel mill.
But the manager
didn't want to give her
a job.

"When I first came here,
you didn't want me,"
said Mattie.
"Back then,
it was because
I am a woman.
Now a lot of women
work here.
Now you won't take me
because I am black.
It wasn't fair then.
It isn't fair now."

Then Mattie
read about a new law
in the newspaper.
Any mill
that was helping the country
fight the war
could not shut out
black workers.
So Mattie went back
to the steel mill.

"I know
you have jobs,"
she said.
"The law says
you cannot shut me out
just because
I am black."

"You really stand up
for your rights,
little lady!"
laughed the manager.

"The law says
I have a right

to work here,"
said Mattie.
"You cannot tell me
that isn't true."

So Mattie got a job
at the steel mill.
But this time,
she wasn't the cleaning woman.
This time,
she did the same work
the men had always done.
The mill
was hot and dirty.
Mattie was 45 years old.
But she was strong.
She surprised herself
at how hard
she could work.

One day
an older white man
came over to Mattie.
"We want you
to join the union,"
he said.

"The white union
or the black union?"
Mattie asked.

"There is
only one union now,"
said the man.
"Blacks and whites
work together
on the mill floor.
Why shouldn't we
work together
as a union?"

Mattie smiled.
"Sure, I'll join the union,"
she said.
"Times have changed.
Now there is one door
instead of two."

"What do you mean?"
said the man.

"Never mind,"
said Mattie.

When she got home
that night,
Mama was singing.
"Nobody knows
the trouble I've seen.
Nobody knows
but Jesus."

"I haven't heard
that song for years,"
said Mattie.
"We surely have had
our troubles,
haven't we, Mama?"

"Yes, child,"
said Mama.
"We have."

"But things are looking up,"
said Mattie.
"I joined
the union today.
One union for everyone.
Mama, do you know
what that means?"

Thinking It Over

1. Why is it so important
   that there is only one union now?

2. Do you think Mattie
   has had more than her share
   of trouble?

CHAPTER 13

Mama sang
"Nobody Knows"
more and more often.
She didn't say much
these days.
She almost never
got up from her chair.
But in her own way
she seemed happy.

"Why do you sing
that song?"
Mattie asked her.

"It makes me think
of home,"
said Mama.
"We always sang it
in the field.
My mama
sang that song.

And her mama
before her.
It's an old slave song.
I don't want you
to forget it, child."

Not long after that,
Mama died
in her sleep.
She had found rest
at last.

Mattie knew
Mama had wanted to be
buried down South.
It would not be easy
for Mattie to do.
But Mama
had come to Chicago
for Mattie.
Now Mattie
could take Mama home.

She took the train.
The box that carried Mama
was in one car.

Mattie rode
in another car.

   At last
they were home.
First Mattie went
to the funeral parlor.
She made sure
everything would be ready
for Mama's funeral.
Then she walked
down the main street.
The old place
had seen little change.
The dirt road
was paved now.
There were
a few new houses.
But most of the old houses
were still there.
They just looked older.

   There, in the middle of town,
was the old sweet shop.
Mattie walked up to it.
There were still two doors.

"Colored Only"
and "White Only,"
said the two signs.
Mattie stopped
in front of
the "White Only" door.
She put her hand
on the knob.
Then she opened the door
and went into the shop.

"Can't you read, lady?"
asked the man inside.

"Where's Mr. Prinn?"
Mattie asked him.

"The old Mr. Prinn
is long gone,"
said the man.
"I am John Prinn, Jr.
Who are you?"

"My name
is Mattie Charles.
I grew up

on a farm near here.
Why does your shop
still have one part
for black people
and one for white?"

"I don't know,"
said Mr. Prinn.
"It's always
been that way."

"Didn't you
ever think about it?"
Mattie asked.

"Not really.
If I changed it now
some white people
would get angry.
They would stop
buying my sweets."

"Don't the black people
get angry?"
Mattie said.

Mr. Prinn
didn't say anything.

Mattie walked out
of the sweet shop.
She was angry.
She looked around.
Other black people
were out on the street.
"Come over here!"
she called.
"Come here!"

One by one,
they came over to Mattie.
A small crowd
grouped around her.
Mattie spoke to them.
"Black people
work and die
in the fields and factories
just like white people do.
My boy's in the war,
fighting for this country.
I'm sick and tired

of 'White Only' doors.
Now, who is hungry
for a sweet?"

A change
seemed to come over
the crowd.
People were talking
and shaking their heads.
Then eight black people
followed Mattie
through the
"White Only" door.
They sat down
at a table
in the "White Only" part
of the sweet shop.
They waited
for Mr. Prinn
to come over
and take their order.

Mr. Prinn
stood behind the counter.
He acted
as if no one were there.

Then Mattie Charles
began to sing.
The other eight people
joined in.
"Nobody knows
the trouble I've seen,"
they sang.
"Nobody knows . . .
nobody knows . . ."

For ten minutes
they waited and sang.
Then Mr. Prinn
came out
from behind the counter.
He walked
toward the table.

"What can I get you?"
he asked.

Mattie spoke first.
"I'll have
a soft drink—
and a sweet roll, too,
if you please."

Thinking It Over

1. What is the meaning
   of what Mattie did
   at the sweet shop?

2. What is your idea
   of "going home"?

3. Would you
   have gone along
   with Mattie's plan?